Danger in the Darkest Hour

Magic Tree House® Books

#1: DINOSAURS BEFORE DARK
#2: THE KNIGHT AT DAWN
#3: MUMMIES IN THE MORNING
#4: PIRATES PAST NOON
#5: NIGHT OF THE NINJAS
#6: AFTERNOON ON THE AMAZON
#7: SUNSET OF THE SABERTOOTH
#8: MIDNIGHT ON THE MOON
#9: DOLPHINS AT DAYBREAK
#10: GHOST TOWN AT SUNDOWN
#11: LIONS AT LUNCHTIME
#12: POLAR BEARS PAST BEDTIME
#13: VACATION UNDER THE VOLCANO
#14: DAY OF THE DRAGON KING
#15: VIKING SHIPS AT SUNRISE
#16: HOUR OF THE OLYMPICS
#17: TONIGHT ON THE *TITANIC*
#18: BUFFALO BEFORE BREAKFAST
#19: TIGERS AT TWILIGHT
#20: DINGOES AT DINNERTIME
#21: CIVIL WAR ON SUNDAY
#22: REVOLUTIONARY WAR ON WEDNESDAY
#23: TWISTER ON TUESDAY
#24: EARTHQUAKE IN THE EARLY MORNING
#25: STAGE FRIGHT ON A SUMMER NIGHT
#26: GOOD MORNING, GORILLAS
#27: THANKSGIVING ON THURSDAY
#28: HIGH TIDE IN HAWAII

Merlin Missions

#29: CHRISTMAS IN CAMELOT
#30: HAUNTED CASTLE ON HALLOWS EVE
#31: SUMMER OF THE SEA SERPENT
#32: WINTER OF THE ICE WIZARD
#33: CARNIVAL AT CANDLELIGHT
#34: SEASON OF THE SANDSTORMS
#35: NIGHT OF THE NEW MAGICIANS
#36: BLIZZARD OF THE BLUE MOON
#37: DRAGON OF THE RED DAWN
#38: MONDAY WITH A MAD GENIUS
#39: DARK DAY IN THE DEEP SEA
#40: EVE OF THE EMPEROR PENGUIN
#41: MOONLIGHT ON THE MAGIC FLUTE
#42: A GOOD NIGHT FOR GHOSTS
#43: LEPRECHAUN IN LATE WINTER
#44: A GHOST TALE FOR CHRISTMAS TIME
#45: A CRAZY DAY WITH COBRAS
#46: DOGS IN THE DEAD OF NIGHT
#47: ABE LINCOLN AT LAST!

#48: A PERFECT TIME FOR PANDAS
#49: STALLION BY STARLIGHT
#50: HURRY UP, HOUDINI!
#51: HIGH TIME FOR HEROES
#52: SOCCER ON SUNDAY

Magic Tree House® Fact Trackers

DINOSAURS
KNIGHTS AND CASTLES
MUMMIES AND PYRAMIDS
PIRATES
RAIN FORESTS
SPACE
TITANIC
TWISTERS AND OTHER TERRIBLE STORMS
DOLPHINS AND SHARKS
ANCIENT GREECE AND THE OLYMPICS
AMERICAN REVOLUTION
SABERTOOTHS AND THE ICE AGE
PILGRIMS
ANCIENT ROME AND POMPEII
TSUNAMIS AND OTHER NATURAL DISASTERS
POLAR BEARS AND THE ARCTIC
SEA MONSTERS
PENGUINS AND ANTARCTICA
LEONARDO DA VINCI
GHOSTS
LEPRECHAUNS AND IRISH FOLKLORE
RAGS AND RICHES: KIDS IN THE TIME OF
    CHARLES DICKENS
SNAKES AND OTHER REPTILES
DOG HEROES
ABRAHAM LINCOLN
PANDAS AND OTHER ENDANGERED SPECIES
HORSE HEROES
HEROES FOR ALL TIMES
SOCCER
 NINJAS AND SAMURAI
CHINA: LAND OF THE EMPEROR'S GREAT WALL

More Magic Tree House®

GAMES AND PUZZLES FROM THE TREE HOUSE
MAGIC TRICKS FROM THE TREE HOUSE
MY MAGIC TREE HOUSE JOURNAL
MAGIC TREE HOUSE SURVIVAL GUIDE